THOMAS & FRIENDS

Percy's New Friends

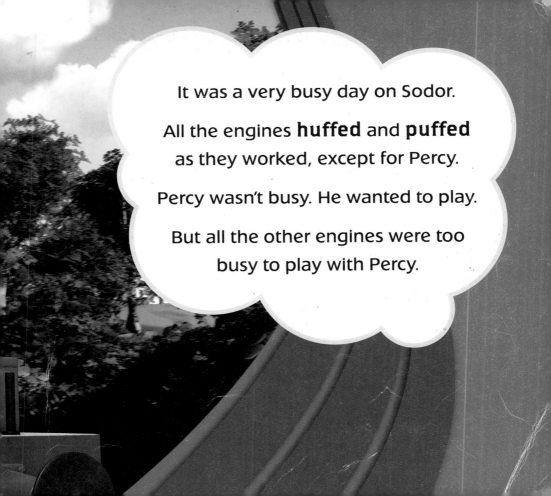

It was a very busy day on Sodor.

All the engines **huffed** and **puffed** as they worked, except for Percy.

Percy wasn't busy. He wanted to play.

But all the other engines were too busy to play with Percy.

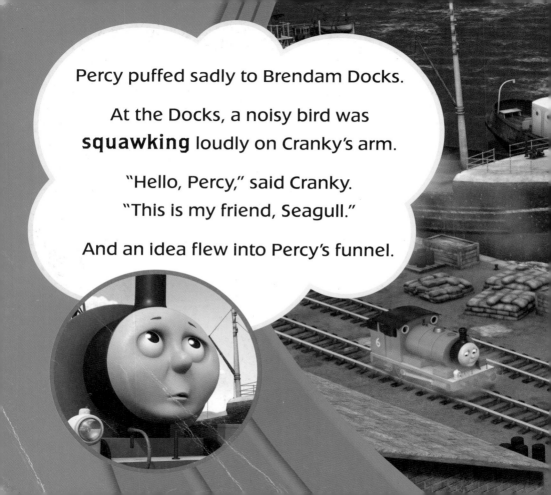

Percy puffed sadly to Brendam Docks.

At the Docks, a noisy bird was **squawking** loudly on Cranky's arm.

"Hello, Percy," said Cranky.
"This is my friend, Seagull."

And an idea flew into Percy's funnel.

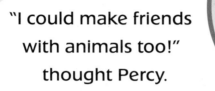

"I could make friends
with animals too!"
thought Percy.

And he **clattered** away
to make some new friends.

The noise scared Seagull and he
flew away!

"Not so loud, Percy!" warned Cranky.
But Percy didn't hear.

Percy puffed into the woods.
He saw a rabbit.

With a *wheesh* and a *whoosh* and a **hoot** and a **toot**, Percy rushed to make friends.

But the rabbit turned tail and raced away into the bushes!

Further down the track Percy saw some squirrels.

With a *wheesh* and a *whoosh* and a **hoot** and a **toot**, Percy rushed to make friends.

But the squirrels scurried away up a tree!

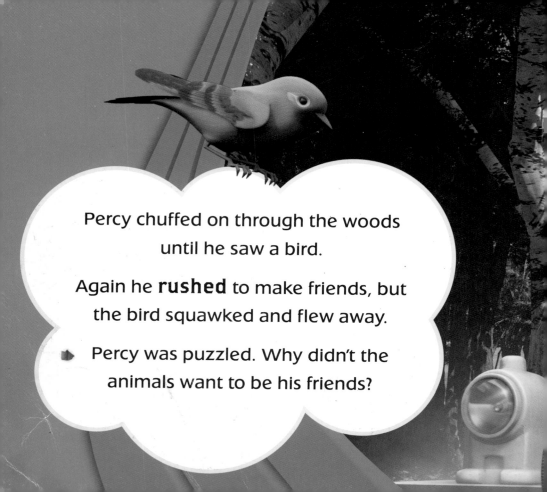

Percy chuffed on through the woods until he saw a bird.

Again he **rushed** to make friends, but the bird squawked and flew away.

Percy was puzzled. Why didn't the animals want to be his friends?

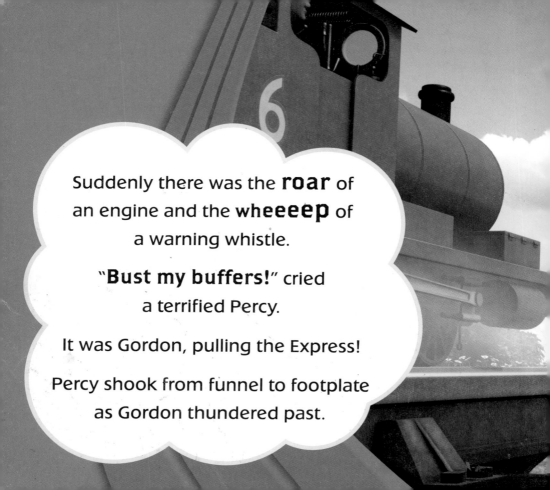

Suddenly there was the **roar** of an engine and the **wheeeep** of a warning whistle.

"Bust my buffers!" cried a terrified Percy.

It was Gordon, pulling the Express!

Percy shook from funnel to footplate as Gordon thundered past.

Thomas saw what happened.

"Are you OK?" he asked Percy.

"I was scared," said Percy.
"Gordon is **big** and I'm only little."

Then an idea **bubbled** up in
Percy's boiler.

Percy set off back
through the woods.

This time Percy puffed **slowly**
and **carefully**. Soon, he
saw the bird.

"Hello," said Percy, quietly.

Cheep, ***cheep***,
replied the bird,
and he flew onto
Percy's buffer.

Percy puffed on **carefully** and **calmly**.

Next he saw the squirrels.

"Hello, Mr and Mrs Squirrel," he said, softly. "I didn't mean to scare you."

The squirrels leapt onto Percy's buffer too.

Finally, Percy saw the rabbit again.

"I'm sorry," said Percy, "I was too loud before."

The rabbit twitched its nose and hopped
up next to the squirrels.

Percy puffed proudly on. He was
the **happiest** engine on Sodor
with all his new friends!

PEEP! PEEP!

The End